The Cynic in Extremis

THE CYNIC IN EXTREMIS

POEMS BY
Jacob M. Appel

ABLE MUSE PRESS

Able Muse Press

www.ablemusepress.com

Printed in the United States of America

Library of Congress Control Number: 2018931560

ISBN 978-1-77349-014-4 (paperback)
ISBN 978-1-77349-015-1 (digital)

Cover image: "Woof Aloof" by Alexander Pepple
(with "pug wrap" by Matthew Henry)

Cover & book design by Alexander Pepple

Able Muse Press is an imprint of *Able Muse:* A Review of Poetry, Prose & Art—at
www.ablemuse.com

Able Muse Press
467 Saratoga Avenue #602
San Jose, CA 95129

In everyone there sleeps
A sense of life lived according to love.
To some it means the difference they could make
By loving others, but across most it sweeps,
As all they might have done had they been loved.

—Philip Larkin, "Faith Healing"

Acknowledgments

I am grateful to the editors of the following journals where many of these poems originally appeared, sometimes in earlier versions:

Ascent: "The Homely Girls"

Blood & Thunder: "Heir to Hippocrates"

Coe Review: "Our Dog Turns Thirteen"

COG: "Those Summer Breakfasts," "The Paper Hanger," "Shrinking with Doubt," "Visiting Alumnus," and "Infidelity"

Crab Creek Review: "Escheatment"

Evansville Review: "Coop" and "The Cynic in Extremis"

Gargoyle: "Transaction Costs," "Flying with Clarity," and "Touring Greenwich Village"

Grub Street Literary Magazine: "Assembling the Exercycle"

Hiram Poetry Review: "Anti-Poem for an Inaugural"

Hospital Drive: "On the Sudden Death of a Beloved Acquaintance"

Margie : "Comedy for the New Millennium"

Midwest Quarterly: "Reckoning"

Mississippi Review: "Murder-Suicide"

Mudfish: "Below Fragile Skies"

Natural Bridge: "1939"

Off the Coast: "Blackberry Winter"

Slippery Elm: "On Holiday"
Slush Pile Magazine: "First Crush"
Stonecoast Review: "Summer Camp Socials"

Foreword

In Jacob M. Appel's *The Cynic in Extremis,* the inevitability of mortality and the capriciousness of its unfolding linger beneath clever, wry, and ultimately mournful lines. In a piece recalling the second wedding of a sister, Appel's speaker muses that at the proceedings "Nothing is said of angelic schemes/ of destiny bound at ensoulment./ No word of who will die first" (15-17). In another, as a neighborhood processes a local murder-suicide, the "... men shudder with their own worst thoughts ... a grip to the throat, a vision/ of their lurking cataclysmic potential" (21-24). The crypt-keeper remains ever-present.

From this masterful collection arises the sense that, with the end so woefully unpredictable and fate so fickle-hearted, to waste any moment amounts to a sin. That may be why Appel's speakers and characters often toil in nostalgia, bemoaning missed chances and misguided choices. Quirky characters, often full of longing and regret, pepper Appel's work, like the uncle so cynical he "steered clear of con games like synagogue/ And life insurance" (4-5) and his compassionate opposite, the pigeon-feeding, environment-destroying Mrs. Z. These characters seem to fail to leave a mark on the world, beyond the poet's eye.

In "On the Sudden Death of a Beloved Acquaintance," Appel's speaker laments:

> . . . Yet unearned grief
> Pools like blood in my throat. So much life
> Squandered on lukewarm associations:
> The tonsured clerk in the post office,
> Our shank-eyed receptionist, Uncle Saul.
> They vanish and the space fills quickly.
> How few leave a lasting hole in the ether. (20-26)

Appel's speakers, repeatedly outsiders or observers, tend to find themselves in the torturous position of a Cassandra, hyper-attuned to the reality that life is fleeting and often ends in confounding circumstances. Yet Appel's speakers are not only observers. They, too, fall prey to human folly and find themselves pondering choices made or unmade, actions taken or not.

"Summer Camp Socials" recalls a childhood dance in which the speaker stood to the sides "like a dunce" (15), only to pass up the chance to dance with another outcast (a balding girl, the target of mockery) like himself, one whose "laughter/ carried across the sultry ether" (22-23). He fantasizes of an alternate past, telling the reader, "This girl stars in the revision of my life" (24). But this collection consistently affirms that life is too short for such revisions.

Of another love interest, a deceased first crush, killed in a fire, Appel writes:

> I will reach for her in the darkness
> Like a boyhood treasure lost behind a sofa,
> Irretrievable, forever inches beyond my fingertips. (21-23)

Here the reader encounters another elegy for a lost chance, for a life that will soon be forgotten.

Crucially, throughout these pieces, a particular chorus of ghosts arises, one that suggests the ancestral beginnings of this familiarity with life's fragility.

"1939" begins as straightforwardly as it ends: the first line reads, "In the courtyard of the yeshiva at Lemberg . . ." (1) and continues on to paint, in vivid detail, a typical day in the community.

The piece concludes by describing two brothers carrying a tailor's dummy together, "Separated only by the beech mannequin/ And the nine months that will determine/ Who walks right and who walks left" (29-31). In a similar vein, the haunting "Precipitation" recalls when "human ash rained across Prussia's heartland" (3) and housewives crossed themselves as children caught "snowflakes on their tongues" (15).

Only a generation or two removed from this chaos and cruelty, the "cynic" in the title of Appel's collection could only be considered quite reasonable. Life can be snuffed out for anyone at any time, a cosmic joke told by a random universe. And yet, in Appel's work, humor and love live in the punch line. Cynicism does not preclude beauty. It neither stymies the pursuit of connection nor stifles a laugh. If anything, our ephemeral nature only enhances our humanity. One can always find delight in the alluring laughter of the irresistible balding girl or in Mrs. Z's unwise but well-meaning feeding of the pigeons, her ". . . sweeping gesture,/ Of unyielding kindness/ That might obliterate the earth" (22-24).

In "Yet," Appel writes: ". . . Temperatures rise./ Foundations Crumble. Nations too..." (4-5), concluding this weary summation of humanity with "Maggots feed on the flesh/ Of schoolgirls. And yet I love you still" (15-16). The world crumbles. It burns. Nonetheless, here in the reader's very hands, poetry exists. Here lives the word, exquisitely utilized, allowing the story of the fickle world to be told.

Brigit Young

Brooklyn, New York
January 9, 2018

Contents

The Cynic in Extremis

Visiting Alumnus

"I once sat in those very chairs," I say,
"Like you," which isn't strictly true,
As I was a rather restive, twitchy scamp
And those low-slung tube steel seats
Must be in their umpteenth incarnation.
But I do recall assembling for visitant
Grandees—a lieutenant governor's aide;
Some under-sung chalk-cheeked fellow
Who'd given his prime and his surname
To novel methods for extracting bauxite.
How the faculty fussed for those men.

Now I have joined their ranks.
All of my own grade school teachers
Dead, or nearly so: Pretty Miss Teal
And plain Miss Kelly and Doc Horton,
Fifth grade, who dressed as Captain Kidd
Each Halloween and later drowned.
Never again will Mrs. Serspinski trap
"A rat" in "separate." How could she?
She'd be well past one hundred.
I had not even realized until now. . . .

And all of those embryonic faces,
As yet untainted: What's to be shared?
Nothing, of course. Or nothing I dare
Divulge: The fleeting ways of goldfish,

Of parents. That all doors exit. Doubts
Festering, awaiting a stubborn, spiteful
Flame that always sparks too late.
Color inside the lines or out.

Summer Camp Socials

We journeyed by decommissioned school bus
To all-girls camps wedged into lakefront
Berkshire notches, most now defunct,
Where Scarsdale bankers sent their daughters
To weave lanyards. Wire poked through
Gashes in the vinyl seats. A toxic residue
Of antiperspirant choked the twilight.

In the makeshift ballrooms—
Gymnasiums, mood-lit refectories,
A converted hay-barn painted mauve—
Slender thighs flashed through clouds
Of Malibu musk. Boys breathed Binaca
Like fire, savored the first fruity tang of
Maybelline kissing potion.

I hugged the corners like a dunce.

At one camp, there was a bald girl—
Pale, lanky, not unpretty—but without
So much as an eyebrow, her pregnant
White scalp latticed with veins. On the bus,
Guys called her Kojak, snotted about parts
She didn't need to shave. Nobody ever
Asked her to dance, yet her laughter
Carried across the sultry ether.

This girl stars in the revision of my life.
I stride across the dance floor on fumes of
Bravado, let her faint waist melt into my
Trembling fingertips. She ripples with joy,
But not surprise, because she has known
I am coming, because she's been waiting.

In my unrevised life, she is still waiting.

Touring Greenwich Village

Spouses of dentists—wives and one husband—and
Only me to guide them. The dentists are in an
Air-conditioned ballroom near midtown, absorbing
The latest advances in articulating paper. I'd expected
The wives—and one husband—to have better teeth.
I had never given consideration to the spouses of dentists,
Which is likely why I agreed to lead this tour.

Walking backward on a summer day is hell on the calves.
Willa Cather lived here, I say. *Sara Teasdale died there.*
Dental spouses nod politely, displaying chipped canines.
I might add: This is where a poet whose name you wouldn't
Recognize wrote about a bridge I could easily sell you.

Next I might say: This is the spot where Hannibal
Led his elephants across the Alps, and over there,
Beyond that bus stop, hunchbacked Richard III,
Who may not actually have been hunchbacked,
Fell to Henry Tudor. And there—yes, right where
You're all standing, brave Pheidippides, proclaimed
The Athenian victory over Persia before collapsing
Fatally onto the asphalt.

At this moment, you spouses of dentists, I feel
Drained as Pheidippides, his marathon complete.
Only that man saved civilization, while I stand
On blistered feet, watching you gawp at me,
With your poor occlusion, your ashy crowns,
Knowing we are leagues beyond rescue.

Concurrences

In the infusion suite
Of this storied hospital,
Which will be scrapped
For condos, I spot
My third grade teacher,
Who will soon be dead.

Carved hollow, yet still
Spring in her smile:
How easily she salved
A bee sting, poultice
Scrapes, found magic
In the dull reiterations
Of childhood.

You will not remember—
Yet she does: down to
That sailor's bucket cap,
The unmatched socks.
Her eyes graze approval
Over my stethoscope.

I have a boy in third
Grade now. Hard to
Believe. While we're
Here, he's studying
Fractions and decimals.

Yes, she says, sprightly,
As though of strangers,
And while I drilled your
Fractions, someone's
Teacher stared up at this
Very ceiling, poison
Flowing through her veins.

Below Fragile Skies

The doomed façade bides unnoticed,
Fractured brickwork dumb,
Gargoyles lurking.

On the sidewalk, tenants buzz and flutter:
Mrs. Pastarnack, who will lose a son in Korea,
Dr. Epps, who will lose an eye to lymphoma,
Skull, our toothless, round-backed super,
Who carries loss like a bowl of stew.
I watch from the bay window.

After midday, threats of the deluge.
Wrappers swirl around trash cans;
A crisp, harried breeze chills the nape
Of Old Rabbi Sellers, soon to remarry.
                                    Then rain.

Gladys Krim skirts the corner,
Oblivious to the rumbling eaves,
Shielding her schoolbooks under her angora—
Doting, homely, mouse-eared Gladys,
Who was to be a neonatal nurse in Pittsburgh,
A godsend to gasping infants—and to raise
Three healthy boys of her own.
She has forgotten her umbrella.

I think often of those children, adults now,
Wondering where they are,
As I hug the curb while I walk.

Coop

Our widowed neighbor, adrift and warped
Like sea-bleached wood, befriends pigeons
And feeds them homemade chicken scratch
In the courtyard. The rat-birds despoil
Rhododendrons and azaleas with droppings.
Diseased feathers speckle the benches,
Float on the shoals of the fountain.
At the core of her maelstrom, Mrs. Z.
Models a gospel of privation.

Drafted as an envoy by the coop board
To shoo off this nuisance, I feign neighborly
Cheer as I wipe off a perch beside her.
She holds her shoulders stiff, neck taut—
Like a royal ibis, or a Nubian stork-god,
Exulting amidst her flock. *When I was a boy,*
I say, *my maiden aunt took me to feed crusts
To geese at a local pond. I thought myself
A benefactor—but I was just clogging
Up their guts and wasting food.*

Pigeons are not geese, says Mrs. Z.
She sows an arc of millet and safflower
Across the slate—a sweeping gesture,
Of unyielding kindness
That might obliterate the earth.

Infidelity

A kiss stolen on the fire escape
And the world does not end.
Bridges fail to crumble.
No clocks strike thirteen.

I am drunk. She is drunk.
Even the kids appear drunk
Although only high on sugar
And inadequate supervision.

A Rubicon forded: like a first
Cup of coffee or joint. For my aunt,
The point of no return is a suicide
Note dispatched through the post.

For my grandfather, nearly a rabbi,
The afternoon his brigade liberated
Buchenwald. Afterward, his god
Neither lives nor dies, but hibernates:

A hydrant waiting for a fire.
Now I am (like him) with no
Insurance, aflame in my belief
That houses never burn.

RMS *Lusitania* Departs for Liverpool

Through a sea of bowlers and boaters and crinoline
Glide the notables—stoop-shouldered Vanderbilt;
Saurian, moon-crowned Frohman, drawing cheers.
Reflected funnels ghost-dance in the uneasy surf.
Brine steams off the jetty. Whistles like bayonets
Saw passage for a neckless matron atop a sedan chair.

Vendors in newsboy caps hawk forty-eight star flags,
Cigars, sprays of oxeye daisies. A steerage-bound girl,
Church-scrubbed, scraggy, whisks past an applecart
In the grasp of her elder sister, her gaze magnetized
By the mounds of polished fruit.

Up soars the gangway! Round grinds the anchor!
Then kisses, champagne, banjos strumming ragtime
Off the quarterdeck. Momentary flutter pier-side
As an electrified phaeton storms the throng like cavalry,
Doors opening in motion. Out flies its imperious,
Mutton-chopped driver, ranting at the harbormaster
While footmen hoist parcels from the carriage. Oaths
Ricochet like grapeshot.

When the apple vendor recalls that balmy morning,
So many decades later, he'll speak of this imperious
Latecomer who catches the final tug out of port.
Some days, he'll cup an apple into the smooth, cool
Palm of the blossoming girl. Some days, his grip
Closes around hers, holding them both afloat.

Trick-or-Treating in Suburbia

How soon dusk settles over the crusted lawns,
And the pinched air, pregnant with frost, whips
At the ears—yet no caprice of wind or time
Can restrain my son, a nine-year-old Galen
Wielding a tinfoil scalpel. For one evening,
He is the real doctor, while I serve merely
As grizzled chaperone. His tiny arms swim
Inside his great white coat.

Our home base is my mother's house—
My boyhood home—a neighborhood chosen
For the proximity of its dwellings. All speed
And fervor, the boy leads me to doorsteps
Which could be portals: here lived Mrs. Blau,
Who left us stewed kumquats on an iron stool
Like poison for raccoons. On the corner,
Eddie Finn's uncle—an orthodontist—
Doled out apples and Johnson's dental floss.

One door opens on Molly Seward's dad,
Still beak-nosed as Ichabod Crane, shuffling
In Velcro-sealed slippers. His hearing aids
Whistle as though calling hounds. A fool
I am to expect recognition.

I do not tell my son: This man's daughter
Crushed my heart (not once, but twice)
In seventh grade *and in ninth*. His wife—
She is both ex and dead—served treats
Of a different sort to your grandpa.

In the kitchen, my mother waits up for us,
A widow in a threadbare robe, curlers twined,
Braced to comb tonight's sweet bounty
For infected needles and razor blades.

She'd have found them years ago,
Had she known where to look.

Escheatment

Every winter we emptied the abandoned boxes.
Come the February bank holiday, our branch manager—
Mr. Teague, my first year, then flint-eyed Mr. Dawson—
Gathered the senior tellers at daybreak
Within the time-lock vault
For a painstaking inventory.

We generally worked in silence, save when confronted
With oddities: a spent artillery shell; nude Polaroids
Of an overweight hausfrau sporting a balaclava.
Someone had wanted to protect these—against fire,
Against nuclear winter. Someone sought to preserve
A receipt from Rizzo's Oyster House, dated 2-21-63.
One box contained a baby's cotton bib.

Too often I matched a name with a face:
Ida Lindstrom, who brought us dove-shaped
Gingerbread every Easter; the palsied pharmacist,
Kovac, who left behind a kaleidoscope and
Pounds of worthless Slovak coins.

                        And one year,
That doddering snake called Babcock
Who failed to understand compound interest,
And twice sought to have me fired: his box
Held only an empty white-gold locket and
And a sprig of verbena pressed in glass.

The Cynic in Extremis

You could never put one over on my uncle.
He whiffed the treachery in Girl Scouts,
Scoured his returned change for Canadian pennies,
Steered clear of con games like synagogue
And life insurance.
His college education he invested in a tire shop,
Listed in his wife's name: Who would send
A woman to prison over taxes?
His breath stank of canned tuna.
His politics lacked mercy.
Alger Hiss? Guilty. Julius Rosenberg? Guilty.
Sacco and Vanzetti? More likely than not.
His gut fed on the raw meat of vindication.
One evening a white girl from the college
Came round petitioning for a pair of jailed teens:
Like the Scottsboro Boys? He echoed.
Boys were probably guilty of something.

I visit him in the old veterans' home.
My aunt is dead. Nobody else will go.
Five-day stubble quills his submerged jaw.
He welcomes me as though I am a Brink's guard
Serving him a sack of wooden nickels.
Of course, you've come, he says,
Slapping his palm against the bedsheet.
You were always a sucker.

Comedy for the New Millennium

Someday the Holocaust will be funny.
Like the Crusades.
Like the assassination of Julius Caesar.
Like Helen Keller reading the waffle iron.
Dentists will tell jokes.
Did you hear the one about the boxcars?
So these two elderly Jews, Moishe and Pincus,
Wander into an extermination camp . . .
Yet jokes—no matter how clever—
Have a knack for turning stale.
Children will groan and beat
Their fathers to the punch lines.

Soon enough, 9-11 will be funny.
Like the *Titanic.*
Like the *Hindenburg,*
A flaming barrel of incandescent laughs.
So these hijackers—get this—
They're going to commandeer four *jets on the same day.*
Did I mention that they're Muslims?
No? Well, they're Muslims . . .
Guests will lean forward, expectant,
Waiting for the coup de grâce,
While sleeve-tugging kids demand,
What's a Trade Center?

Murder-Suicide

We'd adjusted to the hollers, the slingshot accusations
Ricocheting over hollyhocks and peonies. Once,
A squad car after midnight. A torn valise on the slate walk.
Men's clothes strewn across the broad clammy lawn.
Oxford shirts. Briefs. Rumors of a child, barefoot,
Tapping snot-lipped on a neighbor's screen door.

Every night for an entire summer: Fathers,
Stripped to their sleep-shirts,
Lean into the sweltering dark.
Contemplate shouting back. Don't.
Mothers tug tiny hands away from the
Carnage of socks and sweaters.

For months afterward, husbands attend to trifles.
Dishes are washed without asking. Teenagers
Say *I love you* to their parents unprompted.
A nephew appears, takes charge. Instantly,
The mildewed-shreds of menswear vanish.
Painters, in coveralls, rejuvenate the siding.
Do-gooders post letters to the *Star-Standard*
About mental health, gun control. Alone,
Men shudder with their own worst thoughts,
At blows glimpsed but never landed:
A reflexive shove, a grip to the throat, a vision
Of their lurking cataclysmic potential.

Anti-Poem for an Inaugural

I have tuned in to catch the words of the anointed,
Or so I claim, because who among us watches an
Inauguration for the poem? Okay, I suppose there
Are a few—purists who read *Playboy* for the prose,
Who drink whiskey for the flavor. But we measure
Our national pleasure in strikeouts, not stanzas, so
We expect little from the anointed, and little is what
We receive: Robert Frost in various shades of tan.

Nobody invites Langston Hughes to stand behind
The president and speak of dreams that stink like
Rotten meat. Nobody asks Allen Ginsberg to howl.
Nobody atop the alabaster podium of democracy
Wants to hear Anne Sexton tell of Nazis stuffing
Live pigs into her mama's womb. So the rage of
The gagged simmers with tight-balled fists far from
Those perfectly articulated tercets of glossy praise.

Next time, somebody should raise the possibility
That there is no hope left—that it is all used up, that
Our brightest days stand behind us, fleeing with limp
Tails between scrawny legs. Next time, somebody
Should remind us that poetry is dead and the literacy
Rate is higher in Havana. Next time, somebody should
Cut off an ear. Next time, we should all place our
Names in an enormous hat and draw for the open mike.

If there is a next time.

First Crush

That girl who left me breathless—
Once dead to me, now dead—
Extinguished in a house fire in Brighton.
How unremarkable the house looks
On the television screen: the charred
Shutters and flamed-gnawed siding
Ill-fit masks for the discount spool
Of Band-Aid days and carpool years
Trimmed short so abruptly.

The husband is giving interviews.
One hand cradles a photograph
Of this woman whose body he has claimed,
His arm covetous around her shoulders
With the two daughters, Cheryl
And the younger one—half-orphans now—
Posed like war trophies.

He will remarry, of course; quickly too.
Who dares begrudge him that? Because
One can love again, if never as one loved
At seventeen. He will recall her tenderly.
I will reach for her in the darkness
Like a boyhood treasure lost behind a sofa,
Irretrievable, forever inches beyond my fingertips.

Yet

The center does not hold.
Scourges sweep across the weary land
Stamping man's imprimatur on man
In blood and steel. Temperatures rise.
Foundations crumble. Nations too. Fevers,
Fierce and tropical, hemorrhage through the eyes
Of entire armies. Heads on pikes remind us
What has happened and what yet must.
Scalding white dust scorches like a sun.

And yet we are here. In the park,
A woman old enough to be your mother
Hawks half-charred rations scrounged
From the pockets of corpses.
The absence of songbirds pierces the morning
Like a bugle. Maggots feed on the flesh
Of schoolgirls. And yet I love you still.

1939

In the courtyard of the yeshiva at Lemberg,
After a cloistering rain
The boys burgeon and rustle like barley.
Dawn gleams off the high stained glass,
Tabernacle panels yet unshattered.
Swallows nest jittery under the eaves.
At the drinking pump, earnest young teachers,
In fringes and round rimless glasses, steady
The crowns of their homburgs.

Titters of nerves among the pupils. Hormones.
Snickering. Hands thrust into cotton pockets,
Toying marbles, apple cores, slingshots.
The gout-hobbled rabbi, who is only forty-five,
Conclaves with his wife's loud imperial nephew,
Visiting through the autumn from Breslau.

And the streets still with Germanic names.
And the cries of the city:
The egg man hawking, claw-voiced like a fowl;
The horns and tires of motor cars;
The knife shaver coaxing his deaf,
Bedeviled donkey from the muck.

Surely, appear the dawdlers:
Red-eyed, dillydally, tremulous.
A pudgy, indifferent lad kicking pebbles.
Brothers of twelve and thirteen
Sweat-mopped, buoyant, pride-slaked,
That discarded tailor's dummy braced
On their shoulders like a drunken mate,
Separated only by the beech mannequin
And the nine months that will determine
Who walks right and who walks left.

A Collective Endeavor

Anyone on the platform might have taken the shove—
A clipping stroke, really, but enough. Had she not caught
Her uptown transfer, snouting into the car umbrella-first,
That persimmon-lipped waif might have shouldered the blow.
Or the stiff, gabardined businessman toying the skateboard.
So easily we accept that a single contingency leads us
To our fates. Not the failed algebra exam in ninth grade,
The scraped knee hiking Yosemite. A dropped coin.

Too little time, decides the businessman (a rumble stirs
The tunnel)—and yet the strewn body insists to the last,
Lungs lapping, cataracts of blood below a deep-rent temple.
Who can blame the waif for squeezing shut her eyes?
If the woman on the track had chance to muse, she'd say,
How long we have. Until we don't. Which is what a
Young mother will realize briefly, wordlessly, before
Hurrying home to her brood. The pusher—grizzled, hardly
Human—will feel a pure rush of victory from his kidneys,
Although over whom or what he cannot ever say.
A social work intern will give up riding trains.

In the morgue, on the graveyard shift, a junior pathologist—
Unmarried, pushing forty, steering a jaw that protrudes like
The prow of a great vessel—will note the victim's cesarean
Scar, her chestnut nipples. Her boss will trace the contours
Of torpid colon to a shriveled pouch, vestige of a long-burst
Appendix that should have proved fatal. Both will embrace
That timeless statistical canard:

How lucky she was!

Jury Duty

A merciless August morning,
Yet our chamber is frigid
As a post office. Lofty,
Majestic ceilings. Cracked paint.
Walls guarded by the watchful,
Matted eyes of long-dead jurists
In powdered, full-bottom wigs.

The bailiff accepts our lunch
Orders, recommends against fish.

#2 and #9 wish to revisit testimony.
That is treason to #8, red-faced and
Sweating like a whiskey priest, who
Has a business to run, and a hanging
Offense to #6, who voices desperate
Concerns about her parking meter.
The retired actuary, #4, has grown
Drowsy, stuporous. And, all the while,
I am madly in love with #7, stunning,
Chestnut-haired #7, whose father,
I now know, spent eleven months
Locked up for insurance fraud.

My nature and instincts lean
Toward acquittal. #7, who has
Said all of a few sentences in
The four days that I have known her,
Who hardly realizes that #3 exists,
Voices her conviction: *Guilty.*
Instantly I am in agreement, persuaded
By her slight stammer, by the delicate
Goose-flesh of her forearms.

What value is a stranger's life,
Really, when love is at stake?

Learning to Discard

Those early years had been for gathering:
Marbles, teacups, lanyards, truth,
Degrees and lovers, spouses, children,
Space proves boundless in one's youth.

No one warned us that to discard
Wants a fierce and ruthless drive;
Wistfulness schemes with inertia
To keep our treasured hoard alive.

Yet attics full and cellars brimming
Stand no match for frailty's rout;
Mementos yield to winter's tempest:
Take what you want—the rest goes out!

So man accumulates and discards,
Cleaving flesh down to the bone,
Our flights of ego fade to nothing,
Our neighbor's nothing like our own.

Homage to Assimilation

I am the wicked son.
I celebrate the Passover with bagels
And bacon. I play lawn tennis
In white shoes on the Sabbath.
You should see my tattoos.

What are these peculiar customs? I ask:
Nail water. *Kappores.* Circumcision.
Like shackled hands clutching
From the cold dead earth of the shtetl.
That is my ancestral homeland—
Barren tracts of Pale, root vegetables,
Litvak and Galitzianer bickering in Yiddish.
Not some irrelevant patch of Middle East desert
Wrested from strangers. When my forebears
Prayed *Next Year in Jerusalem,* they meant only
A better year in Grodno, in Dvinsk, in Lviv.
The history of my people ended at Sobibor.

Once the swastikas inevitably return
Disguised as budded crosses or lion's heads
Or inverted exclamation points,
I will stand at my mezuzah-free doorpost
Objecting: *Judenrein. Judenrein!*

The last laugh will be upon us both.

Flying with Clarity

Our flight attendant is older than I'm used to—
Maybe the oldest person on the flight, in fact—
Certainly old enough to know better, so when
She announces that my seat cushion can double
As a flotation device, that second mini-amaretto
Urges me to rise like a royal herald and shout, *No,*
It cannot! I mean, has anyone, anywhere, in the
History of aviation ever survived a catastrophic
Failure by floating away on a sliver of nylon?
Jesus Christ, lady, has it never crossed your mind
That steel tubes cruising five hundred miles per hour
Don't just skim the ocean gracefully like cormorants?
No, they sink. Sink, sink, sink! You'd be
Swimming with the fishes around Davey Jones's Locker,
If you survived the impact, which you wouldn't, because
You're old, and out of shape, and not made of graphene.
And if by some miracle you did manage to grab
Hold of your cushion and paddle unscathed through
The field of debris, hypothermia would kick in,
Soon enough, and in three minutes your rheumatic,
Ice-stiff fingers would lose their grip on that precious
Flotation device of yours, and you'd go the way
Of TWA and Pan Am and everyone else in your damn
Line of work who thought themselves unsinkable.

I say none of this, of course. In sit placid as a madman
Doped on Thorazine, nursing my third amaretto,
While you indicate the floor lights that will lead us,
In case of emergency, from this lunacy into
The dark wintry waters beyond.

Assembling the Exercycle

Depicted on the box in pristine gleam,
A resplendent, full-armored steed,
Alluring as Sinon's gift to the Trojans:
I feel ten pounds lighter just admiring
The steel bolts that will lock together,
Harmonized as enzyme and substrate.
A blueprint of dashes steers me forward,
Like a pilgrim pursuing the one true path—
Only that path, it turns out, requires a
Size-three Phillips-head screwdriver,
And using a size-zero for a substitute
Gnaws off the drives. Moreover, four
Pillow blocks and two flange bearings
Connect on the diagram, while the bag
Contains three of each, and no sane
Human being could distinguish a left
Bearing cup from her right companion.
Sweat eats its way through my shirt,
Trickles down my flank. On a trial
Run, the front wheel emits a wheezing
Sound—like an untreated asthmatic—
Followed by a dull moan that recalls
Tortured Puritans beneath pressing boards.
Nameless, unclaimed pieces jangle inside
My pockets, reminding me that I will not
Exert myself so vigorously again until,
Years hence, in a burst of spring cleaning,
I dust the damn machine with a damp cloth
And haul its treacherous corpse to the curb.

Transaction Costs

The postman knows secrets:
Magazines sheathed in black plastic,
Finals warnings, notices of default.
Overwrapped packages that rattle
Pharmaceutically. One morning,
Inside a Ziploc bag, he delivers
A crushed marital aid, all shards
Of fluorescent pink and yellow,
Marked: "Damaged in Transit."

Maybe that is what keeps him going,
Day after day, year after tedious year,
Performing in a role that we never could,
Like collecting coins at a toll plaza.
He slips among us hardly noticed,
Humming on torrid August mornings,
Hirsute brown calves strained and sweat-
Soaked below his regulation shorts.
Sipping from his water canister, he
Lingers beneath an open window.
Our voices, like power, drift to him
On the hot summer breeze.

Reckoning

Some unpardonable transgression—
Paperclips gouged into an electric socket,
Maybe mothballs choking the boys' toilet—
Has led us to this Armageddon:
My parents, togged out as for synagogue
Or a funeral, driving through the dense
October gloom to meet Miss Stoutwald.

Miss. S. is months away from hanging up
Her final paper snowflake and the pumpkin
She wields through the annual Halloween tribute
To Ichabod Crane. I encounter her twice
In retirement: a decade later, home from college,
I will run into her waiting at the bagel shop,
Where she calls out to me by my full name,
And I realize she must have been pretty
In her youth and that her "girlfriend" is actually
Her *girlfriend*. Four more years pass: she
Beams at me from the obit page of the *Post*.

To her, my parents, too, are children.
I ride in the back seat of our Buick,
Which smells of damp beagle and acetone,
Fearing the price that Miss S. will exact
From them for my wrongdoing.

Caveat

Nobody mentioned in this poem
Is based upon anyone, living or dead,
Especially my Uncle Wayne,
A first rate SOB who decked
His own mother one Thanksgiving,
Skimming her dental plates
Over the cranberry sauce,
And who had to be bailed out
By his future ex-son-in-law.

Any resemblance to real persons
Is purely coincidental, including
My fifth grade teacher, Miss Pratt,
Who said *I'd* end up a delinquent
For feeding crayons to her hamster,
And flashing Molly Crandall,
But later surrendered her license
After fondling a twelve-year-old
Girl at a DAR picnic.

Any mention of Amy Pullman,
Who jilted me without a tear,
After I paid her way through
Four years of veterinary school
Might open me up to charges
Of defamation, except defamation
Is false, while Amy actually did
Have a fling with my brother
On the way out—as though I
Care enough to hold a grudge
Or would ever afford that bitch
The satisfaction of uttering
Her blighted name in a poem
Which I have not done.

Blind Date with a Poet

Most poets remain unknown to me personally,
Long dead or distant or too old to engage,
Inexorable precursors like bedrock and telephone wires.

The few I do know from school or cafés
Or chitchat over hors d'oeuvres, prove familiar
And cloying, like my parent's house in the suburbs.

How exquisite to discover the rhythms of a poet
I've never met, but soon will—maybe,
Only once.

Precipitation

Two evenings at the twilight of the war—
For Jews and Germans there is only one war—
Human ash rained across Prussia's heartland.

Or what remained of it.

From the crematoria at Chelmno, a rare north wind
Dappled Elbing's fallow market,
Danzig's scorched husks,
The muddy, shell-struck lanes of Konigsberg,
Where Kant had taught theology to Herder.

Urchins hawked umbrellas door-to-door.

In Karthaus, the Japanese consul, passing
Through by train, wrote to his wife
Of the cherry blossoms at Mt. Daigo.

Housewives crossed themselves as children
Caught snowflakes on their tongues.

Family Tree

Those questions that I thought too late to ask—
Grandma's maiden name, her mother's hometown,
The ship that carried her father from his hard-earthed
Russian shtetl across the Atlantic—all now glower
From my daughter's burgeoning schematic
As ominous chasms.

My wife, a Yankee, once a Protestant,
Is a fifth grade genealogist's idol:
She can trace forbears to colonial baptisms,
Chart cousins, many times removed,
In circuits binding far-slung transistors.

We Jews have only memory to link us.
A voice stilled effaces generations.
A branch forgotten is expunged forever
Like ashes lost to the breeze.

Blackberry Winter

April flutters in on the plumes of warblers,
Whispers through hyacinth lips,
Scents the nursery with lilac and verbena.

My father, near the far cusp of his vigor,
Mulches at daybreak, catalogs tubers,
Transplants peonies into plastic trays.

He keeps one cagey eye on our patrons,
Another upon my future, his only wish
A sham dream that I too may sow.

He laments, washing calloused palms:
The earth wants another poet like a crown gall,
Like downy mildew, like Dutch elm disease.

Then a cruel north wind spites the earth,
Glazes begonia buds, lacquers iris beards.
Azalea strain under a chainmail of ice.

Bundled in winter sweaters, Papa surveys
His lost bounty: all those frost-stiff lilies,
All that squandered hope.

My Sister Remarries

We have trodden this road before
Like alpine ramblers out for a jaunt
Who crash an early blizzard
And circle again to the foot
Of a once numinous peak.

My sister forgoes lace
For a tea-length puce gown
Of no-nonsense gabardine.

Her hand-me-down groom,
Vaunting girth and pate,
Brims bonhomie—too much—
As though captaining a yacht.

A surviving uncle plays
Father of the bride.

Nothing is said of angelic schemes,
Of destiny bound at ensoulment.
No word of who will die first.

Heir to Hippocrates

My father rises from cold-water nothing
To tend the kidneys of stars. In nephrons
And glomeruli, he discovers silver vessels,
Mines gold veins. One year he scores
A transplant for the governor, whose wife
Calls in the nervous dawn to talk
Creatinine and cyclosporine levels.
Gourmet baskets crowd the kitchen,
Signed by billionaires and Olympians.
A-list celebrities call him "Doc."

A limousine, long as a jumbo jet,
Arrives in the darkness to speed
My old man to Washington.
I will come along, he cautions
His joyless, ear-pieced escorts:
Mom is in labor with my sister.
What choice do these men have?
The doc, like Mighty Oz, has spoken.

I must wait in the antechamber,
Surrounded by high-backed chairs,
Under portraits of world leaders,
Chaperoned by a wizened butler
And a buxom, bright-eyed agent.

They claim, she whispers, over my drowsy head,
That he's saved the Pope and Queen Elizabeth.

Her companion shrugs, chuckles.
The queen's valet is still a valet, he says.
I curse his words—but my father more.

Distinctions

Too young to see the faint deep line
Between commerce and affection,
I befriended the milkman, the paperhanger,
The two aging men my grandmother
Paid twenty dollars weekly to vacuum
And scrub. Ed—grizzled, bearded—
Called me "boss," saluting as I passed;
Roy, clean-shaven, boasted an artificial
Incisor green as a pistachio nut. Every
Friday they mopped and scoured, yet
Somehow left the house no cleaner.

One Friday morning, Ed arrived alone.
He lugged buckets from his dog-eared
Packard station wagon—wheezing,
Feet hobbled by invisible chains.

In a Harlem hospital lay his partner,
Stroked-out and mute-struck.

"We should visit him," I urged
My grandmother.

"Adorable, just adorable," she replied—
Repeating the words to my aunt—
Words she'd find again that spring, when
I begged to take an injured songbird,
Who'd thumped her parlor window,
To a veterinarian.

On Holiday

This particular blowup,
Same as all the others, yet distinct:
We've pulled into a Ramada lot
Outside Frankfort, Kentucky,
Or a Motel Six in Georgia.
Someplace between places.

Vacancies—but two stories up.
The lobby's incandescent glare
Cannot blind my mother to the inferno
That awaits us in the darkness: flames
Gnawing through curtains like moths,
Lungs flooding with toxic smoke,
Swan dives from balconies. She
Insists upon a ground floor room,
Voice raised, as though my father
And the clerk, a gum-snapping teen,
Are in conspiracy.

We stop for supper en route
To the next motel. My sister dozes
Into her mac and cheese. Across
Place mats, our parents clasp hands,
Road-raw and heat-sapped. Still capable
Of mistaking peace for joy.

Solid Ground

In the parking lot of the Laurendale Mall
We pause to watch the excavation of a fort
Where colonial militiamen,
Armed only with pride and plug bayonets,
Repulsed a Redcoat onslaught.

On a tarp lay shards of cloudy glass,
Pewter spoons, ramrods, musket stocks.
Guarded by a sweat-stained coed
Half your age.
So young to be so serious.
Like those Pennsylvania farm boys
Willing to die for Mad Anthony Wayne
And a vague sense of honor
And a patch of asphalt behind the A&P.

How pleased these urban diggers look.
As though they've hit bottom.
That's good science too: claim
What you've sought, not more.
Everything below is complication.
Pre-Columbian mounds, mammoth horns,
Time capsules from the Pleistocene.
Much like all above:
A shopping cart marooned on a traffic island.
A discarded aluminum crutch.
Impressions of our feet side by side.

Bad News from God

A girthy pamphleteer at the bus station
Proclaims good news from God.
Not for you.
Not pushing sixty-two.
No more imagined headlines,
Summits with prime ministers;
Not even fleeting, fizzy promises
Inked in yearbooks.

All that remains are snippets
For alumni magazines, then
One final notice.
Survived by. In lieu of.
And maybe the same for everyone,
In their way: holocausts, plagues,
Novel routes to come undone.
Or alone, diminished, days
Fused in an unrecorded dirge
Without affair or consequence.

No news at all.

Our Dog Turns Eighteen

Should we cater a bar mitzvah?
We settle for peanut butter pupcakes,
Pumpkin-bacon crisps. Little need
For a fog machine. It's no birthdate,
After all, no anniversary of arrival—
Just an arbitrary day on the calendar,
Chosen to assuage our ten-year-old,
Now eighteen and away at school.

Eighteen!

That's forty-six thousand dog days,
Nested inside human years
Like Russian dolls. My girl laughs
As I narrate his canine feast:
Tongue, an oiled spatula, slathering
Frosting; metronomic tail wagging
Toward infinity.

Neither knows what is coming.

On the Sudden Death of a Beloved Acquaintance

Frayed white coat slack around your girth,
Pockets lumped with tuning fork, reflex hammer,
Corned beef sandwich cloaked in wax paper,
You might have been the cheese man
At the gourmet market, not our virtuoso neurologist,
And when you harangued the medical students
That first morning—or, at least, the first morning
Our paths clashed—opposite the elevator bay,
Eager minds a-huddle, sponging for wisdom,
I listened to you rail against polio vaccination,
The pernicious influence of fluoridated water,
Marxist conspiracies behind zip codes,
And until that benighted open grin suffused
Your leonine features, I too shared the fear
That, in escaping the psych ward, you'd
Clubbed the real Dr. Forrest to oblivion.

Now you're dead. Not a friend, hardly
A colleague—merely a fellow physician
With whom I shared a sporadic patient,
An occasional joke. Yet unearned grief
Pools like blood in my throat. So much life
Squandered on lukewarm associations:
The tonsured clerk in the post office,
Our shank-eyed receptionist, Uncle Saul.
They vanish and the space fills quickly.
How few leave a lasting hole in the ether.

Variations on a Holocaust

From a veiled window overlooking the Prinsengracht,
Anne and Margot observe the Sicherheitsdienst patrol
Gather on the cobblestones: field grays and peaked caps,
Luster and sweat. A captain with mismatched epaulets.
The girls crouch on dust bags of unsold meat seasoning,
Pulses stampeding, nostrils tickled by stale paprika.
But the Germans storm a different annex—a stone bay
Behind a haberdasher's, where my grandmother hides
Among the surplus corset laces and tailors dummies.

My grandmother keeps no diary. She is a full-blown
Woman—war-widowed—her son shipped to the English
Countryside for safekeeping like a cache of documents
Or royal artwork. Most days she knits—unfinished wool,
Abandoned amid want—a neck scarf to reach her cousins
In America. The haberdasher's daughter comes Tuesdays
With potatoes, water, scurrility. Then the Germans arrive
With clops on the stair planks, clamor. She is surprised:
In the street lurk other annexes, other Jews. Why hers?

Anne rises on a gentle May morning to joyous discord:
Light infantry—Canucks—serenading the long-fought,
Sudden peace. *When the lights go on again,* croon boys
Who know precisely enough Dutch to demand surrender
Or to purchase a ripened cheese. Yet there is no cheese.
Hardly a city. From the steerage deck of the *Carpathia,*
She twigs the scape of the devastation: sheared steeples,
Skeletal facades. Public footage for a private newsreel.
And a throb of horror: her journal mislaid on the quay.

My grandmother sends a letter. Smuggles half a page
Between the missives of two other deportees, matrons
Who share only a point of departure—train passengers
Delayed overnight in an unfamiliar station. A Frisian
Girl carries the note to a work camp in Upper Saxony.
Everything after those scrawled lines is, by necessity,
Speculation: the boxcars from east from Westerbork,
Tattooing, delousing, scabies, rats. Typhus. Expunged
Again when Hungarian capos set Belsen's files aflame.

After the wall collapses—in my family there is only
One wall, *one war*—Papa meets up with the Frisian
Girl in Leipzig. Now she's also a grandmother, wed
To a retired magistrate awash in drink and disillusion.
From memory, she gives voice to all three women—
Unable to recall who penned which farewell. Anne
Outlives Otto, Edith. Margot. Never marries. You
May have passed her adrift in a public park, wearing
The stench of want and pennies on her astringent skin.

Shrinking with Doubt

A torch-eyed girl seized
Mid-breath on a public bus
By the voices of restive gods
Cries out against iniquity,
And I reward her pleas
With 50 mg of Thorazine.

How favored she is to be born
Unto our scientific wonders,
Not into that dark era when
A young Orléans maid, called
By these same volatile gods,
Was set ablaze at the stake.

Of course, Saint Joan saved France.

I dare not ask my patients:
Is this the voice that called
Abraham down to Canaan?
Moses forth from Egypt?
Jesus to Jerusalem?

The girl knows I know her secret:
Satan lurks in a syringe; shot by shot,
We cure ourselves of salvation.

Example

He lectures the medical students on boundaries:
Let's say I'm treating Lana Turner. . . .
In this hypothetical, he soon plans to seduce her:
Funny because implausible,
Implausible because she is dead—
Funnier and less plausible had she been living.
Pin-up girls fall not for doughy, bejowled
Endocrinologists pushing seventy.

Nary a smile among his protégés of Galen,
Their precociously fret-bitten faces
Blank as radishes. Some must wonder
If he meant Tina, not Lana, or maybe
That's a distinction lost. For them
The Beatles, Bing Crosby and Beethoven
Belong to the same generation; Lana
A name made up—or might as well be.
Jane Mansfield, even Garbo fare no better.

Time contracts with distance,
Like shadow beyond a peephole:
Charlemagne and Chaucer cleaved
By centuries, yet both medieval.
His own grandfather had sutured an aide
Who'd once served Meade at Gettysburg.
Remote today as Bosworth Field.
Or nearly so. And when he joined
The faculty, newly minted and wed,
He braced his office door with a chair
Meeting female students. Now only
A pervert might doubt his aims:
The closed door not a boundary,
But a chasm.

The Homely Girls

Three days into the school year—her thirtieth!—
And already she divines the full-grown men and women
Marked to inherit these slight torsos, these paste-slathered
Six-year-old hands. Like Polynesian navigators sighting
Distant vessels in the lap of a single wave, or the crystal-eyed
Field marshal who reads an army's fate, and an empire's,
In far-off plumes of cannon-smoke, she listens as their
Tiny piping voices pledge allegiance to one nation indivisible,
Watches them tell and show tadpoles and shards of mica,
Studies their delicate, implausible features, and she knows
Which among her phalanx of rubber band snappers and nail-biters
Will bring the planets to heel—or will at least try—
And which among her fragile-souled, hope-chocked charges
The universe will grind beneath its wheels like road salt.

In one boy's handshake, she can feel herself purchasing
Aluminum siding, or a late-model Cadillac, or six billion
Pounds sterling of bearer bonds—and she will share these
Impressions on open school night. Other revelations beg
More discretion: her two Michaels, B. and W., a dark,
Mischief-grinned lothario, needing only the dashboard
To start counting his notches, and a rusty mopped tub
With the panache of an embryonic podiatrist. But boys,
Even stunted sops, remain boys. Girls weigh upon her:
Catty, cliquish creatures whose feral friendships will
Sort themselves out along inexorable lines—pretty
And pretty enough and plain. Soon the girls who are

Nearly pretty will drop their necklines, their panties,
Their expectations. The homely girls will steel their
Scorned faces, clench their uninviting lips, and manage
Contingencies. For instance, teaching kindergarten.
Yet she promises them they can yet become princesses,
Her task to protract this fleeting carefree interval between
Who these girls never were and who they never will be.

Snow Again

Raging against the grizzly dawn—
Shoulders burning and cheeks aflame,
Yet the drive still a sea of level white—
I spot a child's nose pressed against
The neighbor's glass. My dormant,
Ice-braced shovel stands a yardstick
By which to measure work undone
And yet undoing.

Only scrapes from my neighbor's dig
Mar our reveries: his child dreaming
Of igloo forts and ammunition globes
While he anticipates a future frigid morn
When his son will grow into his labors,
And he will watch with his own nose
Pressed to the same frost-latticed glass,
Cozy in the pride of a job well-done.

That's the crick with kids and shoveling:
They do for a while. Then they don't.

JACOB M. Appel is a physician, attorney, and bioethicist based in New York City. He is the author of seven collections of short fiction, five novels, and a collection of essays. His short stories have been published in more than two hundred journals and have been short-listed for the O. Henry Award, *Best American Short Stories*, *Best American Mystery Stories*, *Best American Nonrequired Reading*, and the *Pushcart Prize* anthology. His commentary on law, medicine, and  ethics has appeared in the *New York Times, New York Post, New York Daily News, Chicago Tribune, San Francisco Chronicle, Detroit Free Press,* and other major newspapers. He taught for years at Brown University and currently teaches at the Mount Sinai School of Medicine.

The Cynic in Extremis was a finalist for the 2017 Able Muse Book Award.

ALSO FROM ABLE MUSE PRESS

William Baer, *Times Square and Other Stories;*
New Jersey Noir – A Novel

Lee Harlin Bahan, *A Year of Mourning (Petrarch) – Translation*

Melissa Balmain, *Walking in on People (Able Muse Book Award for Poetry)*

Ben Berman, *Strange Borderlands – Poems;*
Figuring in the Figure – Poems

Lorna Knowles Blake, *Green Hill (Able Muse Book Award for Poetry)*

Michael Cantor, *Life in the Second Circle – Poems*

Catherine Chandler, *Lines of Flight – Poems*

William Conelly, *Uncontested Grounds – Poems*

Maryann Corbett, *Credo for the Checkout Line in Winter – Poems;*
Street View – Poems

John Philip Drury, *Sea Level Rising – Poems*

Rhina P. Espaillat, *And after All – Poems*

Anna M. Evans, *Under Dark Waters: Surviving the Titanic – Poems*

D. R. Goodman, *Greed: A Confession – Poems*

Margaret Ann Griffiths, *Grasshopper – The Poetry of M A Griffiths*

Katie Hartsock, *Bed of Impatiens – Poems*

Elise Hempel, *Second Rain – Poems*

Jan D. Hodge, *Taking Shape – carmina figurata;*
The Bard & Scheherazade Keep Company – Poems

Ellen Kaufman, *House Music – Poems*

Carol Light, *Heaven from Steam – Poems*

Kate Light, *Character Shoes – Poems*

April Lindner, *This Bed Our Bodies Shaped – Poems*

Martin McGovern, *Bad Fame – Poems*

Jeredith Merrin, *Cup – Poems*

Richard Moore, *Selected Poems;*
                  Selected Essays

Richard Newman, *All the Wasted Beauty of the World – Poems*

Alfred Nicol, *Animal Psalms – Poems*

Frank Osen, *Virtue, Big as Sin (Able Muse Book Award for Poetry)*

Alexander Pepple (Editor), *Able Muse Anthology;*
                          Able Muse – a review of poetry, prose & art (semiannual, winter 2010 on)

James Pollock, *Sailing to Babylon – Poems*

Aaron Poochigian, *The Cosmic Purr – Poems;*
                         Manhattanite (Able Muse Book Award for Poetry)

Jennifer Reeser, *Indigenous – Poems*

John Ridland, *Sir Gawain and the Green Knight (Anonymous) – Translation*
                    Pearl (Anonymous) – Translation

Stephen Scaer, *Pumpkin Chucking – Poems*

Hollis Seamon, *Corporeality – Stories*

Ed Shacklee, *The Blind Loon: A Bestiary*

Carrie Shipers, *Cause for Concern (Able Muse Book Award for Poetry)*

Matthew Buckley Smith, *Dirge for an Imaginary World (Able Muse Book Award for Poetry)*

Barbara Ellen Sorensen, *Compositions of the Dead Playing Flutes – Poems*

Rosemerry Wahtola Trommer, *Naked for Tea – Poems*

Wendy Videlock, *Slingshots and Love Plums – Poems;*
                    The Dark Gnu and Other Poems;
                    Nevertheless – Poems

Richard Wakefield, *A Vertical Mile – Poems*

Gail White, *Asperity Street – Poems*

Chelsea Woodard, *Vellum – Poems*

www.ablemusepress.com